THE

SAMURAI'S

HONOR

THE

SAMURAI'S

HONOR

Walt Mussell

Cover Design by Killion Publishing

ISBN: 978-0-9992910-3-0

Published by Walter Mussell

For Yoshinori and Naomi Ishihara – You explained why I needed to create this story. I hope you enjoy the result.

Author's Note

Though actual figures and events from history are referenced, this story is a work of fiction.

A Western date reference opens the story as Japan employed a lunar calendar in the sixteenth century, the period of this novella. This is used to avoid confusion, as what might be the "third month" on the lunar calendar could refer to April on a Western calendar.

When the protagonist, Sen, and her sister, Haru, speak of their own ages, they are employing historical convention. Japan, like several other Asian nations of the time, counted life from conception, stating that children were the age of one at birth and then aged with the advent of the New Year. This practice is negligible for adults, but misleading from Western thought when applied to children. For example, a child born two weeks prior to New Year would be one at birth and then two only two weeks later. In the story, Sen is fourteen and Haru is sixteen. By Western methods, Sen is twelve and Haru is fifteen. Japan changed this practice in the twentieth century.

Historical and cultural notes related to this story are listed on a chapter-by-chapter basis in the Historical/ Cultural Notes section on pages 56-58. Definitions of specific words are listed in the Glossary of Terms section on page 59.

When a full name appears in the story, the Japanese naming convention of surname first is applied. The protagonist's mother is just called "Mother" with no mentioned name.

Goami: A swordsmith
Goami Sen: Younger of Goami's daughters
Goami Haru: Older of Goami's daughters
Jiro: Apprentice swordsmith and Haru's intended.
Akamatsu Fumio: Former lord of Haibara Castle

Hinkei of Mikawa: A student trained by the Tosa school in Japan, which painted for the Imperial Court up until 1569 and was known for attention to detail.
Yamazaki: High-level retainer to Akechi Mitsuhide
Ogawa: High-level retainer to Takigawa Kazumasu
Iriguchi: High-level retainer to Shibata Katsuie

The following list notes individuals from history mentioned in the book.
Kuroda Yoshitaka: Lord of Himeji Castle from 1567-1580
Oda Nobunaga: Feudal lord who unified half of Japan.
Akechi Mitsuhide: General of Oda Nobunaga and Lord of Sakamoto Castle (ruins located in modern day Shiga Prefecture).
Takigawa Kazumasu: Deputy shogun of the East and Oda Nobunaga's point person in maintaining watch of the Hojo clan.
Shibata Katsuie: General of Oda Nobunaga and Lord of Kitanosho Castle (ruins located in modern day Fukui Prefecture).

CHAPTER ONE

Himeji, Japan – April 1577

"Sen. Sen."

Fourteen-year-old Goami Sen craned her head. Was her mother calling her? The voice had been faint. Had she imagined it? She closed her eyes and listened. Nothing. Birds chirped in the distance while the breeze whistled through the grass. Nothing else.

Except for the clinks and footsteps from her father's swordsmith shop.

Several footsteps, that is. Somebody important was here this morning. Somebody important enough to need a servant or guard. It must be a high-ranking samurai.

Sen rose and peered over the windowsill again. Father always left the window open for air, unless he needed total darkness. He said he needed darkness to judge the quality of the blade by the color of the flame.

Whatever that meant.

She often asked to see her father's workshop. Father always said no. Too dangerous. Yet he always had guests in fine kimonos visit. Sen often asked to meet the guests. Father said he would think about it, so the answer was no.

Sen was too young, her older sister, Haru, always said. Too young. Too annoying. Too irresponsible.

Too inquisitive, her father would comment, especially for a girl. Sen needed to learn her place.

But Father let Haru in the workshop every day, to bring things to him and Jiro.

Jiro. A lump grew in her chest as she imagined his face. Father's handsome apprentice. Haru's future husband. Sen sighed. Haru was so lucky. She was sixteen. Time for her to be matched with a future husband. Matched with Jiro.

"Sen, where are you?" Mother's voice was audible now.

Sen glanced toward the house. Could she avoid her mother for a few more minutes? Father's guest today must be important. She had to see him. Had to see the fine kimono.

She turned back to the window. Haru entered the principal work area of her father's shop, carrying a tray with five cups. Father, Jiro, and three guests. Sen strained for a better look.

Two of the guests wore swords. One of them stood forward, talking with Father. He wore a gold kimono highlighted with images of flying birds. A goatee decorated his face. A handsome man. He was the important one. The second samurai, dressed in a simple gray kimono, stood at the corner of the workshop, his gaze glancing everywhere. A guard or lower-ranked escort.

Sen massaged her thumbs. A nervous habit, her mother always told her. Should she go find her mother? No, better to stay here. The escort samurai might note her movement and become suspicious.

A third man, one dressed in simple clothes, stood near the samurai. Who was he? Was he a craftsman like her father? Both her father and the gold-clad samurai showed the man respect. Why?

Haru moved forward, offering the cups on her tray. First to the gold-clad samurai, who accepted it, and then to the guard. The other samurai refused at first, but a gesture from the gold-clad one made him accept. Next, the craftsman. Then Father and Jiro. Jiro nodded at Haru, appearing to fight back a light smile. Sen's heart fluttered again. Haru was so lucky.

Her sister looked away as if to hide a blush. Haru had feelings for Jiro. Deep feelings.

Humph. Sen's throat tightened and her breaths grew short. Why did Haru get to be two years older?

Sen craned her head again.

"It is an honor to meet you, Hinkei," the gold-clad samurai said to the craftsman.

"The honor is mine, Lord Akamatsu," the craftsman replied.

Lord Akamatsu. Sen repeated the name in her head. Not a name she knew, but one she wanted to remember.

"Your work is famous," Lord Akamatsu replied. "I hear you have worked for several castle lords and even Lord Oda. Is that true?"

"Several lords have honored me with requests for my work."

"I will spend the next few days with top aides to Lords Shibata, Takigawa, and Akechi. Have you worked for them?"

The names ran together for Sen. Lord Akechi sounded familiar. Some connection with Lord Oda. The other names meant nothing.

The craftsman appeared to be nodding. So did Father. It was going well. Birds chirped in the background, blocking out the words. Sen looked back and closed her eyes to listen. Mother was not calling her anymore. Had she forgotten about Sen?

Not likely. Sen peered through the window. Haru entered again and set one cup on the table, then—

"*Itai!*"

The sharp pain in Sen's ear ran through her jaw and down her neck as she felt herself being pulled back. She grabbed her ear and looked.

Her mother, red-faced and crossing her arms, glared at her as Sen massaged her ear. Sen knew that stare. It carried additional chores, chores that would make Sen regret her actions.

"Anything amiss out here?" Father's smooth voice asked as he looked out the window. "I heard a cry of pain."

"It is nothing," her mother said. "I am addressing it."

Her father smiled. "As I expected. Normally the sounds outside are not so disturbing," he said, eyeing Sen, "unless those sounds are close."

Caught. Father knew Sen had been watching. He always knew. "I am sorry I disturbed you, Father." She hesitated to raise her eyes to face the stern look that awaited her, but finally did.

Her father's stare pierced her like one of his swords. "See that it does not happen again."

"Yes, sir," Sen said, afraid to breathe in his presence.

Her father nodded, flashed a brief smile, and returned to his work. A few seconds passed, and then the murmur of talking resumed. Sen exhaled as she listened, hoping to catch a few words.

Her mother tugged on her ear again, and Sen choked on her own breath. Fear would strike if Sen did not pay attention. Mother liked to make jokes, but she was not laughing now. She tilted her head toward the house. Sen rose and followed. The brief walk dragged like a long blessing from an old Shinto priest.

"I called your name," her mother said as they reached the side entrance. "You did not respond. You did not come. Why did you not listen to me?"

"Sorry, Mother." Sen nodded her head. "I just wanted to—"

"What?" Her mother's gaze grew more intense.

"Watch your father? He is busy. His craft requires deep concentration. You know that."

"He was talking with customers. I wanted to see."

"Only one is a customer. An important samurai named Lord Akamatsu. He and one of his aides."

"Is he the man in gold?"

"Yes, Sen, now come with me."

Sen fell in step behind her mother. Voices sounded from behind her. She stopped and turned, seeing Father and his guests step outside. The man in gold possessed a regal bearing.

"Now, Sen. Close the door," her mother said.

Sen sighed and did as she was told, removing her shoes and then following her mother into the kitchen. "Who is Lord Akamatsu? I have never heard of him."

"He is a former castle lord who lost his castle to Lord Oda."

"Lost? He surrendered his castle?"

"I do not know, but he and Lord Oda made peace."

Made peace? That sounded right. Lord Akamatsu resembled a man of peace. Lord Oda preferred to fight.

"Who was the other man? The one dressed like Father."

Mother smiled. "He is a craftsman. Like your father."

"He wants to be a swordsmith? He looked too old. Will Father be teaching him?"

Her mother shook her head, then motioned for Sen to get a daikon from the bin. "Not like that."

Sen handed the daikon to her mother. "How is he like Father?"

"He is a well-known craftsman, like your father. His name is Hinkei of Mikawa."

Sen pursed her lips together. Mother said the man's name like Sen should know it. "Who?"

Mother shook her head. "I know you are young, but even you should know this name. Hinkei of Mikawa is one of the most accomplished painters in the country. He has done work for many samurai. Your father wants him to paint storage cases for both his tools and swords, and also the entry room for his workshop. Hinkei travels everywhere. It has been three years since his last visit to Himeji."

"Father's been waiting three years?"

"Yes. Now you see why you need to leave your father alone."

"Painting. Sounds . . . fascinating."

Sen's mother twisted her grin into a frown as she sliced the daikon. "With that enthusiasm, I guess we can forget about matching you with any artists when you become of age."

Become of age. "You would send me away?"

"Do not worry." Her mother smiled at her. "A girl who does not listen to her elders gains a reputation." She stopped slicing. "Likely no one would be interested."

Her mother laughed, and Sen crossed her arms. Mother's sense of humor was back. One day, Sen would be as quick with words as her.

"Anyway," her mother said, "do you understand why you should leave your father alone?"

"Yes, Mother." Sen took a breath. "But—"

"But what? What were you really doing?" Her mother's stare drilled into her. "Watching your sister?"

Heat rushed to Sen's cheeks. "Yes."

"Why? Is she doing something interesting?"

"She is serving Father . . . his guests . . . Jiro."

"*Jiro?* I understand now. Leave your sister alone, too. She is sixteen. It is only proper. One day it will be your turn."

Sen looked up, swallowing air as she did. "My turn?"

"Yes, you are fourteen, a second daughter, and a healthy girl. Within a year or two, we expect to receive marriage inquiries. You would be a hard worker at a farm or in a merchant's business. Even with your curiosity, you would still be marriageable."

Marriageable? She had thought of the word herself when trying to see Jiro. Now, with her mother saying it, Sen froze. Her with a man? Farmer? Merchant? "Really?"

"I was not even Haru's age when you grandfather asked if I was available for your father. I was the youngest daughter of a sword polisher. My parents thought it appropriate. Your grandparents used to meet at the shrine with my parents. They offered blessings for the marriage. It seems the blessings worked."

Sen stepped back and glanced out the window at the workshop. No one seemed to be outside. No Haru. No Jiro. No man in gold.

"Sen, pay attention to me. We have much to do. Later, I have errands in town and I need you to come with me."

###

The early-afternoon sun brought warmth to Sen's face as she ran to her mother's side. "Where are we going?"

"Did you not listen earlier? I said we are going to town. We have much to do this afternoon."

"For dinner?"

"Dinner, tomorrow's meals, and other places to visit."

"Where?"

Her mother tsked. "Wait. You will find out soon."

Sen bit her lip as it helped her keep her mouth shut. Mother had a surprise. Best not to press her now. The walk to town took over twenty minutes. Sen tried to keep her mind off Mother's secret destination. She asked questions about Haru, but Mother said little, instead pointing out interesting things by the road.

The crowd along the path grew as they approached the marketplace area. Sen always enjoyed crowds. There were many people to watch and she often became distracted. Some people carried poles between them with goods hanging in the middle. A few groups of men carried palanquins, giving someone rich or important a ride. One group carried a palanquin past her, filling the air with a mix of temple fragrances and sweat.

A nudge from her mother brought her back. "This way," she said to Sen, and they headed toward a side street.

The back of Sen's neck tingled. The number of people on this street equaled the number on the main road. Many seemed headed the same way, but the only thing on this road was a shrine they often visited.

The shrine. Sen's breath hitched. She was in trouble. "Mother. Why here? We only come here for New Year's and the Good Harvest Festival."

Her mother sighed and would not look at her. "To pray for you."

Sen's eyes flew open. "Me? Why?"

"Because you are too curious." She shook her head in a show of disappointment. "It is not appropriate for a young girl. Your father was busy this morning. You could have caused him problems."

"Mother, I am sorry." Sen's eyes teared. She looked down, shoving her foot and straw shoes into the ground as far as she could. She had not meant to embarrass Father. She had just wanted to see who his customer was.

Then Sen stopped. The embarrassment had not been just to Father. Sen's disobedience had also dishonored her mother. "Mother, I am sorry I embarrassed you. I will keep to myself and mind what you say."

Her mother nodded. "I accept."

"Are you only here to pray for me?"

"No," her mother said, smiling. "I am here to pray for Haru, too. Will the gods bless her marriage to Jiro? I also pray for your father. May recognition of his work continue."

"You pray for a lot, Mother. How do you say all that with a bow and some claps?"

Her mother laughed. "I do not. I prepare all my requests. Then, when the time comes, I ask for the blessings of the gods. The gods give what they wish."

"I understand." Sen looked up at the *torii*, the

wooden gate that marked the entrance. A series of steps rose behind it, as it stretched into a large mound. Beyond the entrance, a grove of trees lined the path and blocked the view from passersby. This was the festival place, the place to celebrate rice planting and the New Year. Now her mother said it was time to pray.

Mother was right again. Pray for the blessings of the gods.

"What do you pray for, Sen?" her mother asked.

Sen looked down, shoving her toes into the ground. "I do not think about it."

"Think of your place in this family. Think of your father's place in his craft. Think of what is best for everyone. What should you pray for?"

Sen scratched her chin. "I should pray for Haru?"

"Why?"

"When she marries Jiro, he joins our family. That continues Father's craft."

Her mother smiled. "See? You are learning. There is hope for you. We must enter. Now." Her mother did not glance back.

Sen hurried to her mother's side. They crossed under the torii and climbed the stairs, the trees on each side seeming to rise as well with each step. Several people passed by them, headed back toward the gate. It seemed to be a busy day.

They reached the top step and Sen took in the three small buildings in front of her. A path led between two smaller buildings, one each to the left and right, to a slightly bigger one beyond. A much larger building, the main shrine, rose behind the one at the end of the path. Many people milled about the grounds and on the porch of one of the smaller buildings. Several *miko* worked around the grounds, cleaning them. Sen loved miko. The red *hakama*, the pleated pants, stood bright against the white kimono tops. All the women wore their hair long, tied at the base of the neck and trailing down their backs.

Some wore fancy silk ribbons or clips to set them off. All cared for the shrine.

That was what Sen could do. She could be a miko. Better than being the wife of a farmer or merchant. All the women were beautiful. That would mean Sen was beautiful, too. Her mother and father would be proud.

Or could she? Sen had strands of red hair and the red hakama would bring them out. She ran her fingers through her hair, trying to hide the strands that she knew were there. The red strands made her different. Likely, she would need Mother's help.

"Come, Sen," her mother said, pulling her forward. She followed her mother toward the building on the right where a line formed for people to rinse their mouth and hands. She waited her turn, then grabbed the ladle, eyeing her mother as she did so she would not miss a step. From there, she trod toward another line leading to the building at the end of the path. Time to pray.

Mother always prayed. She must have been a miko in a prior life. She would be proud of Sen's desire to become a miko. She could help Sen dye her hair.

A group of men to the left, heading away from the shrine, drew Sen's attention. The man in gold from Father's shop this morning.

"Mother, look!" Sen gestured at the group.

"Sen." Her mother's tone carried rebuke. "You know better than to point. Only *little* children point, and you are past the age where people forgive such impudence."

"But it is Lord Akamatsu."

"Yes, it is. You are fortunate that he has a kind reputation. He treated your insolence for the child you are, despite your age. Not all samurai would have been so kind."

Samurai. Sen looked. Five men. The gold-clad one, his guard, plus three others. All the men wore the two swords of a samurai. "Are they all customers of Father?"

"I do not know any of them. Based on the clothes of

one man, your father might have visited him instead. Do not stare. Ignore them. Think about prayer and behaving as the gods command."

Mother said nothing more, pulling on Sen's arm as Sen dragged her feet but followed. Father might have visited one of them? Why? Who were these men? People milled about, all watching from a distance as they went through their own rituals. No one dared get closer. Mother was right. Even among samurai, these men must be important. The painter from this morning was gone. Maybe his position was too low to be in their presence.

The kimono of the man in gold still glowed in the sun. She had never seen anything like it. His genial smile permeated the shrine. A kind soul.

Sen glanced at the three other men. One had a face that burned red, like when her father caught Sen messing with his tools. Was he mad? Best to keep her distance, like her mother said. The other two men faced away, but one wore blue and the other a light brown with thin, dark brown stripes.

The red-faced man glanced in Sen's direction. She studied him for a second. He wore a red and orange kimono with dark pants that bunched at the knees. He caught her gaze and stared back. A shiver ran through Sen and she looked at the ground. Mother was right. It was not good to stare.

Her mother tugged on the shoulder of her kimono. "Sen, I told you not to look. Come with me."

"Yes, Mother."

Sen and her mother reached the front of the line, saying prayers and then turning to leave. The samurai had scant moved from where she had seen them earlier, and the people milled about, giving them space. Sen came to a stop.

Three miko were now nearby, sweeping close paths. Another miko appeared to approach, carrying a tray. Of what, Sen could not tell.

"Now, Sen. We need to leave."

"Yes, Mother."

Sen walked along the path toward the exit, images of the samurai still fresh in her thoughts.

Crash.

Sen turned back. Two of the samurai were on the ground, the red-faced samurai and the blue-clad one. A miko was also on the ground, the tray and items sprawled nearby. The miko hurriedly rose to her knees and then bowed low, her forehead hovering inches above the ground as the two samurai stood. Two more miko rushed forward and joined the other miko on the ground. They raised their gaze to offer small towels, then bowed their heads low while keeping their hands high.

The red-faced man glared at the miko and raised his hand. The two miko on the ground tensed, ready to take whatever was coming.

Lord Akamatsu and the brown-striped samurai stepped forward and stopped him.

Sen sighed as the red-faced man appeared to grow calm. He could have drawn his sword and struck the woman. Lord Akamatsu dusted the red-faced samurai's kimono while chatting with the blue-clad samurai, who was brushing himself off and chatting with the one in light brown stripes. The brown-striped one, clean-shaven, said some things to the red-faced man, who now nodded. The blue-clad one smiled, his thin mustache now pointing up, took the proffered towels, and passed them to the others. All cleaned their hands and dropped the towels on a tray offered by the miko who brought them.

The miko with the towels glanced in Sen's direction. Her hair was different, tied with ribbons to the side instead of in back, making her hair curl below her chin. Pretty. Sen grabbed her own hair and tried to mimic. Could she do that?

The miko smiled and shuffled off back toward the principal building.

The samurai with the red face remained. He glared at Sen.

Sen froze. Caught staring again. Mother was right. She would cause herself trouble.

The man in gold then turned. Lord Akamatsu smiled at Sen in recognition and seemed to chuckle. He tugged on the sleeve of the red-faced man. The man looked away.

Phew.

A tug on her own sleeve drew Sen to the left. Mother frowned at her and then bowed toward the samurai, apologizing for Sen. Sen turned and bowed low. She glanced at her mother, who frowned at her again, then tilted her head toward the exit. Time to leave.

Sen kept her eyes front as they walked along the path, descended the stairs, and then turned left back toward town. The glare of the red-faced man pressed on her mind. Sen inhaled and steeled her courage. "Sorry, Mother."

"It is not good to stare, Sen." Her mother's tart voice drenched Sen in guilt. "*Especially* at a samurai."

"Lord Akamatsu remembers us, Mother."

"Better that he forgets us. Hopefully, the other three men will."

"Father will be angry with me."

"Your father gets angry about little. Do not worry. Time to go to the market."

The walk to the market took another fifteen minutes. Sen thought of nothing but Lord Akamatsu. "Mother, where was the painter?"

Her mother eyed her suspiciously. "Why do you ask?"

"I thought he was traveling with Lord Akamatsu."

"He is likely visiting with another potential customer. He will return to our place later this week. You must behave when he returns, as much as you must when Lord Akamatsu visits again. Much better than you did this morning."

"The painter is not a samurai."

"That does not matter. He is an artist, like your father.

You *must* treat him with respect."

Sen nodded and said no more. Her thoughts returned to Lord Akamatsu. She must behave as if every customer was him.

Or bring her family shame.

CHAPTER TWO

"You were quiet last night," Haru said as she pulled a weed from the rock garden. "You have said nothing since you and Mother returned from the market yesterday. Is something wrong?"

"No. Nothing."

"Did Mother give you a lecture?"

Sen's chest tightened, sending pain to her face. Could she avoid Haru on this? Not likely. She would find out anyway. "Yes, she did."

"Because you were spying on me and disturbed Father?" Haru asked, then leaned in and grinned. "Or were you staring at Jiro instead?"

Sen glared and crossed her arms. "I was not watching you or Jiro. I just wanted to find out what everyone was doing," she said with a stare before backing up. "I am tired of being left out. But the lecture was not about you."

Haru looked at her with that older-sister-no-lies glance. "Really? I heard you and Mother yesterday."

Sen kicked the ground and turned, unwilling to face Haru. "Nothing. Nothing like that."

"Well, what was it about?"

Sen pressed her lips together, wanting to hold the words in. "We stopped at the shrine before going shopping. We saw Lord Akamatsu there."

"I see," Haru said, holding the last tone. "Did you stare at Lord Akamatsu?"

"Mother thought so." Sen turned and faced her. "There were also three other samurai there."

"Including Lord Akamatsu's assistant, who was here when Lord Akamatsu was here?"

"No. These were three other men. They wore fine clothes, just like Lord Akamatsu. Then there was an accident."

"Accident?" Haru's tone rose.

Sen explained the story about the collision with the miko and how one samurai had almost struck the girl.

"Maybe the men from yesterday and the ones here today."

"Today? I did not know."

"Jiro told me. He mentioned that there were a few important samurai coming today, from two or three different provinces. They are coming to examine Father's work. A messenger arrived late yesterday to request Father's time."

"I did not see a messenger."

"You were too busy sulking," Haru said with a pouty look.

"Who are they?"

Haru pursed her lips. "Jiro did not say. Only that they are important."

"As important as Lord Oda?"

"Nobody is as important as Lord Oda."

"Why are you not helping Jiro today?"

Haru's gaze narrowed into anger. "Because of you yesterday."

Sen looked at the ground. "Sorry, Haru."

"Do not worry. If you wish, we can still see them."

"Without being seen?" Sen sighed. "If Mother or Father catches me again, they will punish me."

"Yes, so follow my lead. You are young. You still make noise."

"I am not that young. You are only two years older than me."

Haru gave her that stare again. "You are fourteen only because you were born just before the New Year, but you will always be younger than me." She leaned in closer. "Listen, little sister, I can teach you one thing," she whispered.

"What is that?" Sen kept her voice soft. No reason for Mother to think they were not busy. Or disturb Father.

"How to sneak around without getting caught."

"How do you know?"

"How do you think I see Jiro as often as I do?"

That was true. Haru sometimes disappeared at night. Mother and Father had yet to stop her. "Will Mother notice if we leave the rock garden?"

"She will call our names first. We must listen for her."

They crept to the other side of the workshop. Sen glanced toward their neighbor. Horses neighed as the old man who lived there brushed them while his grandson, Kochi, played nearby. A gentle kid. Sen had often observed Kochi, wondering what it would be like to have a little brother. He sometimes came over to play when his grandfather was busy.

"Move," Haru said in a hushed tone. "Stop staring at Kochi."

"Coming." Sen ambled, still following Haru and watching her own steps. It would not be good to make noise now.

Haru reached the window and glanced inside, then motioned Sen to approach. Sen looked through the crack left open to allow air.

The red-faced man. He was here.

Sen ducked below the window. She remembered

how the red-faced man had raised his hand toward the miko. He was not a man to disturb. Next to the red-faced man was another samurai. Recognition dawned on Sen. The brown-striped samurai from yesterday. Another man was also there. Thin. The mustached man in blue? Hard to tell, but it must be. Two more men stood in the corners of the room. Guards? One of these men must be as important as Lord Akamatsu.

"Sen, what is it?" Haru asked.

Sen pressed her finger to her lips. *I know them,* she mouthed.

"Who are they?" Haru whispered.

She ducked down. "The samurai from yesterday at the shrine. The ones who were with Lord Akamatsu. They are the ones meeting Father."

The telltale *suu,* the scraping sound of a sword being drawn from a wooden *saya,* resonated in Sen's ears. Mother always said drawing a sword sounded like a sliding door being opened, but there was a difference between doors and swords. If drawn for battle, Father said it made an abrupt *shu* sound, but Sen had never heard such. She imagined it as a quicker slide.

Another *suu* filled the air, followed by polite sounds of admiration. "Lord Akamatsu was correct," a voice said. "Master Goami, your work is exemplary. I know of no other maker of your experience."

Sen's heart warmed, despite the tension in her chest. Praise for her father's work made her proud.

"I am honored by your words, Yamazaki-*sama,*" Sen's father said.

Sen rose again and tried to peer closer. Just the passing of sheaths, blades up, but scant movement or words.

Haru leaned in. "Anything else?" she asked.

"Nothing. They are looking at the swords Father keeps for show."

"Are you sure it is the same men you saw yesterday?"

"Yes, the red-faced man. It is him."

"We heard you have Hinkei coming to paint," another voice said, rising.

"Yes," Father said, "he was here yesterday and will return in three days. He is visiting merchants in town today and tomorrow and has an audience at the castle with Lord Kuroda the following day."

"Move," Haru said. "Let me look."

Sen moved left and strained harder to listen as Haru took the position.

"I know Hinkei well," the voice continued, "he has served Lord Oda and the lords of Yamazaki and Ogawa here. We will visit the castle in two days. I am certain we will see him. As I mentioned to all yesterday, Hinkei never forgets a detail in his work. He can even sketch likenesses of people he has met only once. You are fortunate. Yamazaki? Ogawa? Do you remember him?"

A chorus of *hai* sounded in response.

"Is Jiro there?" Sen asked.

Haru tilted her head and gazed at Sen. "Why does it matter, *little* sister?"

Sen bit her bottom lip as her sister once again rubbed in her age. "Well, I was—"

"What are you doing?" a squeaky voice asked.

Sen's skin chilled, and the two girls turned. Kochi stood there, smiling at Sen.

"Kochi," Sen whispered. "Keep your voice down."

"Why?" Kochi asked again, his voice loud.

"Be quiet, Kochi," Haru said.

"Voice down," Sen echoed, "stay quiet."

"But why?" Kochi asked again.

"Answer the boy's question," her father said.

Sen turned. Father's stern gaze bored into her.

Sen bowed low, pulling at her fingers as she did. "I am sorry"—her throat went dry—"to have disturbed you, Father."

"Stand up," her father said. "Both of you."

They both rose to face him. Sen quivered in place, her head down.

"Look at me," her father said.

Sen raised her gaze but did her best to avoid looking her father in the eyes. He stood rigid, arms crossed in front of him. Behind him stood the other men, all showing quizzical irritation.

"Now," her father said, "my question remains. What were you doing? Haru, stay silent. I want to hear from Sen."

Sen shoved her foot into the ground, hoping she could make a hole and drop herself in it. "We wanted to see who your visitors are. Your customers are always important people."

"Sen. Haru. Come in here. Now."

Sen and Haru nodded, and then they hustled inside. Their father met them in the entrance room. The three samurai stood behind him, spread out and looking serious. The red-faced man, dressed today in light green, stood forward of the three. The thin-mustached samurai and the clean-shaven, round-faced one both wore the same blue and brown-striped kimonos they had worn the day before. All three wore gray hakama, the samurai seven-pleated trousers. Two more men stood behind them, dressed in simple brown kimonos tucked in the back of their sashes. Guards for one of the men here. Only the red-faced man wore different clothes today. He must be important.

Sen and Haru bowed low. "Sorry for disturbing you. We just wanted to see who was here."

"Children interested in a parent's work," the mustached samurai said. "It is, at least, laudable."

"I remember you," the round-faced samurai said. "You were at the shrine yesterday. You are everywhere, young lady."

"You remember me?"

"Yes, it looked like you were with your mother."

Sen's heart fluttered. *He remembers me?* "I am

honored that you noticed, sir."

He smiled at her. "I notice children. I have two daughters of my own. Little details are a fascination of mine."

"Welcome, sir." She looked back at her father and bowed low again. *Remain calm.* As if she could.

"So, you were at the shrine yesterday?" the red-faced man asked, his tone cutting like a blade against Sen's fears. This was no man to trouble.

Sen bowed again. "Yes, sir."

The red-faced man shook his head. "Distance is best." His voice was gruff. "Especially for girls."

Sen bowed again. "I am sorry we disturbed you, samurai-*sama*."

The mustached man chuckled. "Do not be harsh, Yamazaki. I hope to have children someday interested in my activities."

The brown-striped samurai smiled. "My daughters seldom show interest in anything I do. For you, young lady, I have one word of advice."

"Yes, sir." Sen trembled at the kind man whose face now wore scorn.

"You are coming of age, passing the time where people forgive mistakes. Impertinence is never welcome. Inquisitiveness, however, can be made to serve one's lord. Always strive to serve one's lord." He paused and looked at her father. "A plan is necessary."

Father nodded. "Agreed."

"With your permission, Father?" Haru asked. Her father nodded and Haru tugged on Sen's sleeve. Time to leave.

The two bowed and turned to go. Sen's back burned, as if someone's gaze remained on her. It must be the red-faced man, the one called Yamazaki. Why was he staring?

"Tell your mother to keep both of you busy with chores until dinner. I am certain she has plenty of work for both of you."

"Yes, Father," they said as they reached the exit.

Sen put the broom away and glanced at the back entrance. Mother had long stood there but stood there no more.

Gone? At last. She sighed. Mother likely believed she would spy on Father again. Not today. Not ever.

A day had passed since Sen and Haru had disturbed the samurai. Mother had kept both of them busy, saying that they needed to learn their lesson.

Lesson learned, Sen thought.

She viewed the yard one more time. Satisfied she had missed nothing, she headed toward the front of the house.

Haru awaited her on the front step, arms crossed, tapping her foot. "Mother said you and I would finish around the same time. What were you doing?"

"Mother kept checking on me. Made me nervous. I kept thinking I missed a spot somewhere."

Haru stifled a chuckle. "Mother always pays attention to the way things appear outside. The rock garden. The bushes. She cares as much for the house as Father does for his swords. We need to go."

Sen nodded, and the two of them began walking to town.

Ominous clouds blanketed the sky as the sweet scent of impending rain filled her nose. They had to get Mother's task done soon. "What did Mother want us to find?"

Haru rolled her eyes. "Do you never listen, little sister? She needs needles for sewing."

"I remember now. Needle seller." Sen giggled. "Sounds simple."

"Never simple." Haru rubbed the coin Mother had given her, drawing Sen's gaze to it. "Needle sellers are always moving around, calling out and looking for customers. We have to find him."

"That could take some time?"

"Yes. Mother may want us out of the house." Haru stared into space. "Maybe she is trying to get rid of us for a while."

"Why would she do that?"

That all-knowing-sister glance reared again. "Because we interrupted Father. Maybe more customers are coming today."

"To get us away from the house then. Where should we go first?" Sen asked.

"The cloth stores. There are several of them at the edge of the food district, next to the sake shops."

Sen kicked her straw shoes into the ground, pushing the edge of the tie against her toes. Sometimes, it felt like they were slipping off her feet. She knelt to press them.

"What are you doing?"

"Making sure we can move quickly if we need to catch the needle seller."

"No need," Haru said, shaking her head. "If we call out for the needle seller, I am certain he will come."

The walk to the cloth stores took nearly an hour. As they passed through various sections of town, they ran down the side streets. No needle seller. They would meet again at the center and continue forward.

"We are not having any luck," Sen said.

"Well, we are not yet to the cloth stores," Haru responded. "Maybe soon."

Sen looked up, noting Himeji Castle in the distance. A beautiful place. She hoped to visit it someday. Father had visited, providing his services to Lord Kuroda. He said it was no place for a young girl.

The clouds behind the castle appeared darker than they had earlier, as the earthy smell of impending rain grew. Sen pointed the clouds out to Haru. She signaled her acknowledgment, and they quickened their pace. Ahead, a crowd milled about, checking out restaurants and food carts. Maybe they could find a needle seller here. Lots of customers. One booth sold noodles. Others sold fruits and vegetables. Sen and Haru searched the crowd and then each looked down opposing side streets, returning to the center.

Nothing.

They passed the food carts and seafood and seaweed shops, their stomachs growling as they did, and then came upon shops on each side with cloth barrels hanging, announcing completion of a batch of sake. The spring batch must be popular. Customers milled in front of both buildings, making it hard to look around them. No needle seller. A stone lantern and a tax office marked the food district's edge.

"We are about to reach the cloth district," Haru said.

Sen nodded, glancing up as tiny droplets touched her cheeks and hands. The rain was starting. Even if they found the needle seller soon, the storm would drench them on the way home.

They began searching the cloth district. The area was also busy with customers while merchants removed goods from poles and tables, trying to sell as they did and still protect their wares. Sen looked farther down the road. The castle was several hundred yards away. Fewer people in the streets, but they looked official.

No needle sellers in sight.

Not good. If nothing here, then they would have to start over.

Haru indicated the first cloth shop, saying she would ask while Sen stayed behind. The owners would respect Haru. She was old enough. For Sen, they would make her wait.

Haru flitted to the first two stores. Nothing. The third one offered hope, saying a needle seller had been there moments ago. Had they missed him in the crowds? Had he taken another side street they had yet to check? Haru pointed to two side streets, suggesting Sen check one side while Haru would check the other.

"We will both check. If we cannot find each other,

we will meet at the stone lantern," Haru said.

"Yes," Sen answered, sighing as another drop struck her hand. She watched Haru go one way and then headed down the first street. Nothing there. She doubled back and headed to the second cross street, dodging crowds as she hurried ahead.

More drops struck her face, owing to a light breeze. *Last street.* She quickened her pace.

A sudden movement toward the end drew her attention. A flash of metal reflecting remaining bits of sunlight piercing through the clouds. Needle seller?

A loud clink and Sen froze in place, pulling at her fingers as she did. Two figures, fighting. She approached slowly, watching her steps as she did.

Another clink.

Sen drew closer. Two men fighting, one man masked and armed with a short sword. Another man throwing things and trying to flee but nowhere to go. The two men circled. The bleeding man's face became visible.

Hinkei?

The attacker ran Hinkei through. He inhaled and clawed the attacker's face, ripping away the mask. Blood trickled down his cheek and over an odd circle tattooed on his neck.

"Sen, what are you doing?" Haru asked.

Sen turned to Haru, putting her finger to her lips. "*Shi—*" she hissed softly.

Thunder cracked, and rain began to fall.

Haru gasped, her eyes wide open as she appeared to see the attack. Fear covered her face.

The attacker turned and locked his eyes on them.

"Sen! Run!"

CHAPTER THREE

Sen grabbed Haru's hand, and the two hurried back to the main road. They moved left, dodging through the crowd, which scattered to get out of the rain. They ducked under an awning, trying to lose themselves among several adults. Muffled conversations sounded around them.

"This way," Haru said.

They ran into a sake shop. Hopefully, Father would forgive them. Father did not approve of sake. Uncle drank too much. It had taken his life.

"Hey," the store owner yelled as Sen and Haru dodged customers. "What are you doing?"

They both ignored them, sliding a door open and heading into the brewing area and warehouse.

"Why are we going here?" Sen asked.

"The shop is big," Haru said. "Many places to hide."

Sen and Haru ducked behind a storage shelf and headed toward another room in the back. Voices called out, searching for them.

"Will they find us?" Sen asked.

Haru's lips flattened. "Eventually, but it will take

time. Once they are back here, we can talk to them."

"Will they listen? What if they call an official?"

"Even better. We can tell them about Hinkei and what we saw. They will protect us. They will take us home. We will be safe."

A tug on Sen's shoulder turned her around. A man grabbed her shoulders and stared into her eyes. Her body quivered. She looked at Haru. Another man had her sister.

"What are you doing here?" the man holding Sen asked.

Sen struggled to speak and found her throat dry.

"Sorry, sir," Haru said. "We need your help."

Both men relaxed their grips but took positions to prevent Sen and Haru from fleeing. Haru stepped forward and bowed, fluttering her eyelashes the way she always did to get Jiro's attention.

The tension in the man's face eased. Haru's beauty had a way with all. For once, Sen did not mind Haru getting their mother's looks and not having red strands of hair.

The two men looked familiar. Had she seen them when shopping with her mother? The older man, who had gray streaks in his hair, stared at them. "You are the swordsmith's daughters, are you not?"

"Yes, sir," Sen said. She tried to smile as she found the strength to speak. "Our apologies for upsetting the harmony of your shop."

"Your father is an honorable man. What help do you need?"

Haru relayed the incident.

"Take us there," the older man said.

"Can we get the magistrate first?" Haru asked. "The man may still be out there."

The man with gray streaks nodded and glanced at the younger employee. "Fetch an official."

The younger man headed toward the rear of the shop and departed through the back door. About ten minutes later, he returned with a serious-looking man behind him. The official wore a simple brown kimono with dark lines and a single sword in his girdle. The standard attire of those who worked at the magistrate's office. Sen and Haru bowed.

"Thank you for coming," the older man said.

The man grunted.

"We were fortunate," his employee said, "there was already a crowd near the body and two officials. When I told them I had two eyewitnesses, this man came at once."

Sen trembled as the official's gaze held her still. Even Haru's eyelash flutters would not influence this man. They both relayed their stories.

The man listened and nodded. "Come with me."

The girls fell in step, following the man out of the sake shop's rear entrance and back toward Hinkei. The rain had slowed to a light drizzle, but the black clouds remained. Puddles marked the street. Sen glanced around, her stomach twisting. Was Hinkei's killer nearby?

They reached the place. A small crowd had gathered. A grunt from the official parted them. Hinkei's body was still there. Three more men in brown kimonos with dark lines were nearby, searching the area. One of them looked in Sen's direction and walked toward them.

"Wait here. Do not move," the first official said.

The men conferred, while glancing back at Sen and Haru. Were they in trouble? The second official came to them. "You saw what happened?"

"Yes, sir," Haru answered, as she and Sen bowed. "We saw the man who killed Hinkei."

Another official joined them. The men looked the same to Sen. The oldest of them, the one questioning Haru and her, grew even more stern. "Describe him."

Haru and Sen again gave the details. The men nodded in response. The new official, the youngest, turned toward Haru. "So you grabbed your younger sister, ran to safety, and then asked for us. You are a dutiful girl.

You must do your parents proud."

Haru smiled. "Thank you, sir."

Another man dressed in the same brown-kimono style rushed up to the three men. He was younger than them, likely a few years older than Jiro. "Inspector, a word."

The gray-streaked man stepped away, and the two conferred. He glanced back to Sen and Haru. "Did you say the attacker had a circle tattoo on his neck?"

"Yes, sir."

He again spoke with the other man, then turned back to Sen and Haru. "Come with us."

Sen's chest tightened, and she glanced at Haru. Haru raised her gaze. "Come with you, sir?"

"Yes."

"Did we do something wrong, sir?" Sen asked.

"Sen," Haru interjected, her voice tinged with rebuke, "you know better than to question officials."

The official looked at Sen, his face somber. "Your sister is right. You did nothing wrong. For now, come."

Sen and Haru grabbed hands, walking with the junior official and the gray-streaked one. Sen wanted to know where they were going but kept her mouth closed. The walk took ten minutes, crossing the main road and going back toward the center of town before taking another side street, again dodging puddles. Another group of officials appeared ahead, busy talking to each other.

An acrid smell brushed Sen's nose. Sen choked back a gag.

Another body lay there, clad in soaked, blood-stained, familiar clothes. The officials parted, and the gray-streaked one motioned for Sen and Haru to get closer. "Is this the man you saw?"

Sen gasped and studied him. The circle tattoo. The scratches on his face. "Yes, sir. It is him."

"And you?" the man asked, staring at Haru.

"Yes, sir. This is the man who killed Hinkei."

"That is one murder solved. We have two more to go, though we do not know who this man is yet."

"Two, sir?" Haru asked. "Someone else was killed?"

"Yes," the gray-streaked man answered. "We found a young woman this morning. Only a few years older than you. Beautiful girl. She had dimples and a mark under her eye."

Sen inhaled sharply. "Was she a miko, sir?"

The men stopped and stared at her. "How did you know that?" the gray-streaked one asked.

Sen wrung her hands as her heart raced and perspiration trickled down her back. "It was something I remembered. My mother and I were at the shrine two days ago. I saw a miko there who looked like that. She collided with a group of four samurai."

"Who were the samurai?"

"Lord Akamatsu and three other men." Sen searched her memory for the names. The red-faced man was easy to remember. "One was Yamazaki-*sama*. I do not remember the other two."

"Are you certain it was these four men?"

"Yes, sir. Lord Akamatsu visited my father's sword shop. So did the other three."

"At the same time?"

"No, sir. Lord Akamatsu was there two days ago. The other three came yesterday."

"Was anyone else with these men when they visited your father?"

Sen thought hard. Lots of questions. Why? "Two other samurai. Guards. They stood away and did not talk."

"How about with Lord Akamatsu?"

"He had one guard."

"Anyone else?"

Sen paused and looked down. "Hinkei, sir."

"Hinkei was with Lord Akamatsu?"

"I do not know, but they were there at the same time."

"I understand." The gray-streaked man looked at

Haru. "Take your sister home." He turned to the officer who had met them at the sake shop. "Escort them home. Report to me after you do."

The first officer nodded and gestured they should leave.

"We can make it on our own, sir," Haru said. "We have been too much trouble already."

"I insist," the gray-streaked man responded. His tone brooked no argument.

Haru grabbed Sen's hand and gave it a good squeeze, and the two of them headed for home. Sen looked back. The officer was there, maintaining a few steps behind and glancing everywhere. Was he looking for something? Why did they need an escort?

They walked about twenty minutes, and then Sen sidled up to Haru. "Why is the official following us?" she whispered.

Haru hummed for a second. "For our safety, I think. Is he still there?" Haru stared at Sen.

Sen glanced back and then snapped forward. The man's stern face sent chills through her. Earlier, he had been smiling. Why so serious now? Kind of like her father. Sometimes, while working, Father could be happy and laughing. Other times he was serious. It meant he was busy or had a job he needed to do. Did this man have a job to do?

Hinkei's killer was dead. What else was there?

A chill scurried across her skin. *Who killed the murderer? Who killed the miko?*

Another thirty minutes and the girls reached home. The clouds remained, but daylight waned. Sen sighed, as much from exhaustion as relief. They turned to the official and bowed. "Thank you, sir. You honor us."

"I will speak with your parents and make them aware of your assistance. Where are they?"

"Father is likely in his workshop," Haru said, lowering her voice to sound adult. "Mother is probably inside the house, worried about us."

"Unnh." The official's grunt sounded as if he was thinking it over. "I will speak with your mother first."

The official strode to the door and pulled the bell rope. Seconds passed, and then the door opened. "Where have you two—?" Mother paused and looked at the official. "Welcome, sir. Is something wrong?"

"Your daughters have had an eventful day. We detained them as witnesses to a crime. The senior inspector wanted to make sure that they reached home."

Mother's face flattened, and she stared at the man. "I am grateful."

"I would speak with you and your husband."

She looked at Sen and Haru. "There is food in the kitchen. Eat something and then go to the rock garden and scan for weeds before the sun sets."

"Mother, we did that earlier," Sen said.

Her mother's eyes flashed, and Sen retreated. "I noticed some that you missed. Look again. Once you are done, sweep the house."

"*Hai*," Sen and Haru answered together.

They rushed to the kitchen and ate rice balls and then headed back to the rock garden. Voices sounded from inside the workshop.

Several minutes passed. "I would love to listen," Sen said, "but I am afraid."

"We should be. Get back to work."

It grew darker as Sen and Haru looked one last time for weeds. Nothing. Time to go inside. They turned toward the house.

"Ah, there you are," a familiar voice said.

Sen and Haru turned. The gray-streaked inspector approached the house.

Sen's heart raced again. Why was he here?

"Welcome, sir."

"Where are your parents and my officer?"

The girls pointed toward the workshop. They

watched as he entered.

"I wish we could listen," Sen added, pressing down on her stomach as it churned. Food would be good.

"Are you possessed by the fox?" Haru asked, her tone on edge. "We should find something else to eat and then sweep like Mother said."

A long time passed as they continued to sweep. "I have an idea," Sen said.

"What?"

"Ask Jiro."

Haru looked down her nose at Sen. "Jiro?"

"Yes. He will tell you anything. Wear that white braid in your hair and flutter your eyes like you always do."

The look on Haru's face made Sen smile, though her glare spit daggers. "What would look even better is that wooden hair clip Jiro gave me, but I cannot find it." She paused and stared at Sen. "Do *you* know where it is?"

Sen glanced down, brushing her feet on the floor. "Yes," she said sheepishly, going to a closet and pulling out a box of treasured items. "I wanted to see how it looked on me, so I borrowed it." She handed the clip to Haru.

"It is fine to *borrow*," Haru said with a loving look. "Just put things back. I will try to see Jiro tonight. Maybe he will know what is happening."

Sen rolled on the futon, waiting for Haru to return. Once her parents had gone to bed, Haru had snuck out to meet Jiro. Sen had listened to the bug calls echoing through the window, counting the minutes.

Finally, Haru stumbled in. Her smile now gone. Her face ashen. "Sorry, Father rose and checked the workshop. I had to hide until he left."

"What did Jiro say?"

Haru looked down, as if the words clogged her throat. "They found a note on Hinkei's killer. The note directed the assassin to kill Hinkei. It was signed with the kanji *akira*."

"Why is that important?"

Haru drew 明 on the floor. "Do you know this kanji?"

"Yes. That is *akira*. So what?"

"It can also be pronounced *aka*. It is the first kanji in Lord Akamatsu's name. The police plan to arrest Lord Akamatsu."

CHAPTER FOUR

Sen faced the morning with a heavy heart.

Two nights ago, Haru had told her of the intention to arrest Lord Akamatsu. Yesterday, the samurai had addressed business at Himeji Castle.

This morning they would return, under the guise of commissioning Father for work on several swords.

Mother had kept her and Haru at home yesterday, avoiding the chance of either of them letting the news slip. Sen had struggled all day to contain her tears. Hard to believe that Lord Akamatsu could be responsible for the deaths of Hinkei and the miko.

She set out the trays, staring at her mother as she did so. "Mother, can I help Haru carry the trays to the guests? She has too much to carry."

Her mother stared back at her. "Do not go near your father this morning."

"Yes, Mother."

Sen said nothing more and continued to follow her mother's directions. Mother said little, only that Father's work this morning required that he be left alone.

For Sen, this meant watching officials drag Lord Akamatsu away.

"Stop daydreaming, Sen," her mother admonished. "Everything will be fine. Grab the broom and sweep the paths in the back."

Sen nodded and left, heading to the storage shed attached to the back of the house to grab a broom, and began sweeping. Haru passed her, carrying a tray, and then returned within five minutes.

"Anything?" Sen asked.

"Nothing," Haru replied.

Jiro strode across the grounds, his arms swinging. He glanced toward Haru, his eyes bulging wide, but kept his gaze straight ahead.

"What happened?" Sen asked. "He looks angry."

"Father realized I knew. He is upset with Jiro for telling me, but I sense something else. Father is nervous."

"What is Jiro doing?"

"He is telling Mother he will carry the tea to our guests and distribute it. We are not to go near the workshop. No women."

Sen sighed. "Are the police here?"

"They have been here since before dawn."

Sen's heart sank. "What are they going to do?"

"From what I heard before Father made me leave, they will ask Lord Akamatsu to admit his guilt. They will ask him to remember his honor as a samurai in case he disagrees."

Voices rose from the street near the front. Lord Akamatsu appeared at the entrance, flanked by the other three samurai. Sen and Haru moved toward the shed, hoping to avoid being seen.

The four men passed, talking happily. Two more samurai, the guards, trailed them.

Sen's heart fell into her stomach, yet her body felt empty.

Haru turned and looked at Sen. "You are crying."

Sen brushed at the corner of her left eye and wiped away the tear. "I am not crying." She sighed. "I just cannot believe it."

"You are fourteen. You need to learn. We are girls. We listen to our parents. We listen to our officials. When we get married, we listen to our husbands. It is the way."

Sen looked at the workshop. "It does not seem right."

"You are too young to suggest what is wrong and what is right."

"When can you suggest?"

"When you grow up."

Sen looked back at the workshop. Her body tightened into steel. "Then I will listen."

Haru grabbed Sen's shoulder. "You are not going over there."

"Lord Akamatsu is a kind man. I know he is. Something is wrong."

Haru glared at her. "This is too important. You must stay here."

"You are right. It is important. That is why I have to go."

Haru grabbed Sen's wrist and pulled her closer. "You do not understand. You interrupted before. If you do it again, someone could take your head. It is their right."

Sen felt at her neck. "They would do that?"

"I do not know, but it will embarrass Father. Do you want that to happen?"

"No." Sen kicked at the ground. "But I must do this. I know Lord Akamatsu is innocent."

Haru sighed. "You are going to get us in trouble anyway, I see."

The corners of Sen's mouth went up. "You agree?"

Haru nodded. "No, but I will protect my little sister."

They brushed their hands on their clothes to eliminate the dirt from their fingers, then crept around the building to the other side. A quick glance to the neighbors' property. Kochi was nowhere in sight. Yet.

"What if Kochi or his grandfather sees us?" Sen asked.

"I noticed them earlier. They have gone out for a horse ride. They always make it a lengthy trip."

Sen and Haru inched to the side of the house. Voices emanated from the window, growing louder as the two girls drew closer. Sen kept her gaze on the ground, her breath coming in quick gasps. A stray twig crack would rob them of surprise.

"You will need to come with us, Lord Akamatsu," an official said. "On your honor as a samurai, I ask that you come quietly. We will accord you all rights and privilege due your rank."

"You can present your evidence now. That is also due someone of my rank and privilege." Akamatsu's voice was rational and calm. "Your witness is wrong."

"A miko from the shrine told us everything. The incident at the shrine was a ruse. The dead girl confided it to another miko after it happened. You passed a message to the miko. The miko was a courier and passed it to Hinkei's assassin."

"That is not what happened," Sen said.

Sen sank to the earth as chills ran through her while her blood pulsed like a galloping horse.

Haru stared at her. "What were you thinking?"

Sen's mouth dropped open, but she could not respond.

An official appeared at the window. "In here. Now."

Sen rose but kept her glances downward, as she and Haru got in line and headed to the entrance. It was only a few seconds until they reached Father, enough time for her life to flash before her eyes. The look on his face said it all. She would be punished for a long time.

If she survived this act of insolence.

"I have told you to mind your place," her father said. "We will discuss your disobedience later."

"Yes, Father." Sen dared not look up. She had

embarrassed him. She would get a reputation. Father would, too. It would not be good for Father and his business.

"Young girl," an official said, "what did you mean when you said, 'That is not what happened'?"

Sen's hands shook. She massaged her thumbs and took a deep breath.

"Daughter, answer the question."

She kept her eyes down. "I saw the collision between the samurai and the miko."

"And?" the official said.

"The miko did not touch Lord Akamatsu."

"Look at me," the official said.

Sen raised her gaze.

The official tilted his head. "Explain."

Sen took another deep breath. "The miko crashed into the mustached man. Lord Akamatsu did not touch the miko."

The official looked at the mustached man. "Is this true?"

"No. The girl must be faulty in her memory. There was much going on there. She could not have seen everything."

"The girl is correct," Lord Akamatsu said. "I never touched the miko."

"You are wasting our time," the mustached man said. "You would have us listen to the ravings of an insolent child?"

"I would," the local official said.

"The word of a childish girl is irrelevant against a samurai. Besides, we have the note signed by Akamatsu. Evidence enough."

"Yes, we have the note given to the assassin," an official said. "We also have another note, a message received late last night, informing us of the discovery of the body of Ogawa, the aide to Lord Takigawa."

Shu! Shu! Shu!

The mustached man froze.

Lord Akamatsu and Yamazaki-*sama* moved as one.

Two slashes.

The mustached man sank to his knees, then hit the ground face-first, his sword clattering on the floor.

CHAPTER FIVE

Sen put away her futon and headed toward the kitchen, stopping by the window to look at her front yard. She glanced up and down the road beyond. Nothing. Two weeks had passed since what happened with the mustached man. She looked every morning at the road, hoping to see Lord Akamatsu. He had to return eventually for his sword, the one he had requested of her father, but it could not be ready yet. She strained her eyes to see farther. Nothing. Farmers carrying food to market, two over the shoulder and two on a cart.

Two weeks ago still seemed so fresh.

At least Lord Akamatsu was safe.

Something would happen today. Yesterday, her father had mentioned a surprise. She had rolled on her futon almost all night, hoping that Lord Akamatsu would return. How far along was Father on Akamatsu's sword? Had he finished early? Was it at the polisher? Was it getting a special handle? Where was it?

Was she looking in the wrong place? While putting away her futon, she thought she had heard voices. What if

Lord Akamatsu was already here? She should check the workshop.

She headed toward the back.

"Sen," her mother said, bringing Sen to a halt. "You should have joined me in the kitchen. I told you when I roused you that I needed your help. What are you doing?"

Caught. "Nothing, Mother." Would her mother accept her lie?

A door from the back slid open, interrupting her thoughts. Her father stared at her. "Daughter, I have need of you."

Sen nodded as her heart sped. Would this be the surprise? "Coming, Father."

Her father smiled. "We have two visitors. They are here to see you. My good wife"—he looked at Sen's mother—"is the tea ready?"

"It will be ready soon."

"Good. Sen, come with me."

Sen hurried to the back door, following her father into the sunlight.

And froze.

Lord Akamatsu stood there, dressed in a light green kimono patterned with squares and diamonds. A beautiful woman dressed in a blue kimono decorated with an intricate flower pattern stood by his side. Two samurai stood behind them.

"Lord Akamatsu," Sen said, her voice trembling at a higher volume. She bowed low. Dizziness swam through her head and she struggled to stay standing. "Welcome, sir."

"Raise your head and look at me," he said as a polite command.

She obeyed, her gaze flitting between him and the woman to the right. "Yes, sir."

"Young Sen, it is good to see you again."

"Thank you, sir. Good to see you, too."

A chorus of chuckles erupted as if her statement had

been funny. Akamatsu turned and uttered some words to the two samurai behind him. Both men smiled and then resumed their looks of stone.

"Show our guests inside," her father said.

Sen opened the door wide, then rushed to the *genkan* to get slippers for Lord Akamatsu and the woman. They stepped inside. Haru appeared, bringing cushions and offering them to the guests. They accepted and each took a seat on the floor. Haru then brought a tray and a stand. Mother followed with the tea and a rice treat. Both guests nodded.

"You are kind," Lord Akamatsu said. He gestured toward the woman. "This is my wife. The last time I was here, she was visiting with the wife of Lord Kuroda at Himeji Castle. I am fortunate she is with me today."

Sen went to her knees and bowed low, then sat back on her feet, inching away. She could sense Haru doing the same. Akamatsu exchanged a few words with her father as he and Mother sat to enjoy tea. Sen remained hunched on her knees, ready to serve at the slightest request, and leaned forward to listen.

"Sen," Lord Akamatsu said, "you can hear better if you move closer. Besides, we need to talk about you."

Sen's hands quivered. Talk about her? What could this nobleman have to discuss with her? She moved closer, setting herself next to her mother, with Haru next to her father. Sen bowed low, her nose hovering above the tatami floor. "I am at your service."

"I know that," Lord Akamatsu said. "Raise your head."

Sen complied, touching her thumbs as she dared not look him in the eyes. A flick of his hand sent the message. Glance up.

"You have already been of service to me," he said.

"I only told the truth," Sen replied, her voice shaking.

"You did us proud," her father said.

She took a deep breath. "Who was the mustached

man?" Sen asked, glancing between her father and Lord Akamatsu.

"An assassin," Lord Akamatsu said. "He killed the real Ogawa and then impersonated him."

"Why?" Haru asked.

Lord Akamatsu's lips thinned. "The officials found a note on the fake Ogawa, instructing him to assassinate both me and Yamazaki. The senior investigator believes the note was sent by Akechi Mitsuhide, one of Lord Oda's generals."

"Will they arrest Lord Akechi?" Sen's mother asked.

"No." Lord Akamatsu's face grew still. "There is no proof. His closeness to Lord Oda also protects him."

"I thought Yamazaki-*sama* worked for Lord Akechi," Haru said. "Why would Lord Akechi kill him?"

"To remove suspicion from himself. It is hard to know. It is also a guess. The fake Ogawa may have been trying to frame me for Hinkei's death, but he made a mistake."

"What mistake?" Sen asked.

"Sen," he looked at her, "how well do you know your kanji?"

"I am learning, sir."

"The *akira* kanji used in the note has what other pronunciations?"

Sen's chest grew tight. "It is *aka*, sir, like your name."

"Anything else?"

Sen sighed. "I do not know."

"Haru?"

Haru looked thoughtful. "I do not know another pronunciation either, sir."

Father sighed. "I have neglected you both. It can also be pronounced *ake*."

"Correct," Lord Akamatsu said. "The first kanji in my name Akamatsu is also the same as the first character in the name of Akechi Mitsuhide. The police suspected there was more happening than they knew."

"Why kill Hinkei?" Sen's mother asked.

"The fake Ogawa knew of Hinkei's reputation for detail. He knew Hinkei would recognize him as an imposter."

"I am happy that you are free, Lord Akamatsu," Sen said. "Where are you going now?"

Lord Akamatsu glanced to her father and mother, who both smiled back. "I have a new mission. A separate messenger from Lord Oda has arrived with wonderful news for me."

"What is that?"

"Lord Oda has placed me back in charge of Haibara Castle. It is the castle I surrendered to him, so I am grateful to return. I will assume my position there shortly."

"A great honor indeed," her father said. "Do you agree, Sen?"

Sen felt herself smile. "Yes, I agree. Were you surprised?"

"I was," Lord Akamatsu responded. "The castle may have been the reason for the assassination attempt. Confidants of mine informed me that Lord Akechi wanted Haibara Castle and may have sought to remove me, though no one is sure."

"Is it the size of Himeji Castle, sir?"

"It is a little smaller, but it is a grand place. I am honored to be its master once again."

A grand castle. Sen had often admired Himeji Castle. One could see it from many places on a sunny day. What wondrous people must live there, she often thought. Surely Haibara was the same. "It must be an amazing place. You look happy."

"I am, but now I have something to ask of you."

Sen swallowed hard. "Me, sir?"

"You impressed me, young Sen. When you thought I was in trouble, you risked yourself to defend my honor. A samurai lord can receive no greater service. Do you understand?"

Sen breathed deeply. The praise made her dizzy. "Yes, sir."

"Good, as I am here to request that your service continue."

Sen looked up. Continue? "How?"

Lady Akamatsu inched forward. "Would you like to see Haibara Castle, Sen?"

Sen felt her eyes grow wide. "See it? You mean visit and go inside?" Sen sat up straight as her body tingled. "Yes."

"Visit?" Lady Akamatsu said. "This will be a little more."

A little more? "What do you mean?"

Her mother moved next to Sen and patted her hand. "You are a second daughter and old enough, Sen. It is time."

"Time?" Sen asked.

"We want you to come with us, Sen," Lady Akamatsu said. "You will serve us at Haibara Castle and report to me. Would you like that?"

Leave?

Leave her family? Leave Himeji? "Today?"

"Not today," Lord Akamatsu said. "I need to go there first. My wife will return in one month and escort you. The sword I requested of your father will be ready by then. Your father's spirit will travel to Haibara with you."

Haibara. An amazing castle. Her parents were right. It was time.

"I accept," Sen said, bowing low. "I pledge myself to you, Lord and Lady Akamatsu."

"Good," Lord Akamatsu said. "I have a gift, then, to mark this agreement." He reached into his kimono and pulled out a necklace. At the base of the necklace hung a kanji made of wood. A simple ideograph.

She held out both hands, palms up and pressed together, to accept. "The number ten, sir?"

"Yes, it looks like the kanji for the number ten, but

no. It is a cross. It is the symbol for my faith. My wife and I are *Kirishitan*."

Sen rolled the cross in her fingers. "Must I become a Kirishitan, too?"

"No," he said. "The choice is yours."

Lord Akamatsu and his wife rose. The two samurai who had been standing nearby closed toward them. "We must depart. Sen, we look forward to having you at Haibara Castle. See you in a month."

Sen rose and bowed again, as low as she could. To serve a castle lord. It was as high an honor as she could ever hope for.

Sen grabbed the shoes of Lord and Lady Akamatsu and set them at the front door. Lord and Lady Akamatsu nodded their approval, then slipped on their shoes and headed to the street, their samurai guard close behind. She watched as they reached the street and turned toward town.

Toward Haibara Castle.

Toward her future.

If you enjoyed this story, please continue reading for an excerpt from The Samurai's Heart, the follow-up to this work. The excerpt follows the Historical/Cultural Notes, Glossary of Terms, and Acknowledgments sections.

Historical/Cultural Notes

Thank you for reading my novella, *The Samurai's Honor*, the prequel to my novel, *The Samurai's Heart.* The need for a prequel arose due to one comment on The Samurai's Heart from two long-time friends that there was no historical basis for the female protagonist of my novel, Sen, a craftsman's daughter, to be living in a castle eighty miles from her hometown. I wrote *The Samurai's Honor* to provide a reason.

I endeavor to make my stories as historically accurate as possible. Please email me with any mistakes you find. Historical/cultural notes on the story are listed below on a chapter-by-chapter basis. Definitions of specific words are listed in the Glossary in the next section.

CHAPTER ONE

Good Harvest Festival – Sen is referring to an April festival in Himeji where the citizenry prays for a good rice harvest. The festival includes deity offerings for the year's crop as well as ceremonial horses with costumed riders.

CHAPTER TWO

"Nobody is as important as Lord Oda." – Haru's statement is that of a young girl who lives in a domain controlled by Oda Nobunaga. From a history perspective, she is correct. However, in 1577, several samurai lords are vying for power. Nobunaga is having the most success.

Japanese onomatopoeia – Terms such as *shu* and *suu* are forms of Japanese onomatopoeia. Onomatopoeia is much more important in Japanese than in other languages and represents not only sounds but also feelings, movement, and states of being. Despite its prominence, it is rarely used in Japanese literature (outside of *manga*). It is used here to accentuate Sen's age.

Himeji Castle – Himeji Castle is known worldwide as a white, six-story structure meant to represent a heron in flight. It is a UNESCO Cultural Heritage site and one of best-known structures in Japan. Himeji Castle, as it stands today, is the result of a remodel from 1601-1609. This story takes place in 1577. At that time, Himeji Castle was nowhere near its present height. It also may not have been white. Many castles in that area of Japan used black lacquer for reasons of humidity and possibly political reasons. As I could find no reference to definitively support that the castle was black in 1577, I left it white.

CHAPTER THREE

Red strands of hair – Japanese people are known to have black or dark hair. Red strands are an uncommon trait.

Japanese bedding – The beginnings of bedding that resembles the modern futon started possibly around the mid-sixteenth century, though sources vary on this topic. Around this time, thin cotton bedding appeared along with quilt-kimono hybrids that evolved into quilts.

CHAPTER FOUR

None

CHAPTER FIVE

Lord Akamatsu Fumio – The main samurai in this story is based on Takayama Ukon, a prominent Christian daimyo of the late sixteenth century. For Catholic readers, Takayama was beatified in 2017 and his first Feast Day was February 3, 2018. His names include Dom Justo

Takayama and Iustus Takayama Ukon.

Haibara Castle – Haibara Castle, the castle awarded to Lord Akamatsu at the end, is fictional. It is based on Takatsuki Castle, the real castle governed by Takayama Ukon. The incident of the fictional Lord Akamatsu stepping down and then being reinstated by Oda Nobunaga at his own castle is based on a similar incident that occurred in 1578, a year after the time period of this novella. The reason this story occurs in 1577 instead of 1578 is that in my novel, *The Samurai's Heart,* I mention that Sen left Himeji ten years prior. I had to make the timeline match.

The number 10 – The kanji for the number ten is 十. This is why Sen asks if it's the number ten when Lord Akamatsu hands her the cross.

Glossary of Terms

daikon – A large white radish used in several Asian cuisines.

futon – A thin, traditional bedroll that can be folded and stored daily.

hakama – Seven-pleated skirt (trousers) primarily worn by samurai.

hai – The Japanese word for "yes."

itai – The Japanese equivalent of "Ouch" / "Ow"

kanji – The modified versions of the borrowed Chinese characters used in Japanese writing.

kimono – A traditional Japanese garment that resembles a loose robe.

Kirishitan – The Japanese word for Christian.

miko – Shinto shrine maiden

- sama – An elevated term of respect. The better-known term of -san does not exist in this time period.

saya – A thin wooden scabbard for a sword or knife.

shi- - The Japanese equivalent of "shhh."

shu – The sound of a sword being drawn for battle.

suu – The sound of a sword being drawn slowly from a wooden scabbard.

tatami – A straw mat floor covering where the length is twice the width, roughly six feet by three feet.

torii – A traditional Japanese gateway normally found at the entrance of a Shinto shrine.

Acknowledgments

In writing my first novel, *The Samurai's Heart*, I thought I had covered every possible historical issue. As I mentioned in the previous section, friends of mine in pointed out that in *The Samurai's Heart*, I state that Himeji Castle and Haibara Castle are eighty miles apart and that Sen had gone to work there at a young age, an improbable premise. They suggested I needed a good reason for Sen to be at Haibara Castle. So, with my spending a lot of time at home this spring, I penned this story from Sen's childhood. Thank you to Yoshinori and Naomi Ishihara for your recommendation as well as your continued assistance with research questions. I hope you enjoy the story.

Thank you to Dianna Love and Tina Radcliffe for your help, suggestions, and continued mentorship.

Thanks to my online group, Authors of Asian Novels, for your support, research answers, and good wishes.

Thank you to Kyle Cummings and Michael Rofe for your review of my manuscript and your comments. Thank you also to Kim W. Moore, who, as someone who raised four daughters, provided great insight on Sen and Haru to this father of two sons.

Thank you to Amy Knupp at Blue Otter Editing for the edits and to Kim Killion at Killion Publishing for the cover.

Continued thanks to the many Japanese historians whose works I read to ensure my details are correct. Any historical or technical mistakes in this book are the fault of the author.

Lastly, thank you to my wife, Motoyo, and my sons, Andrew and Christopher, for putting up with me when I'm writing.

Please read on for an excerpt from *The Samurai's Heart*. I hope you enjoy it and will consider picking up the full novel.

THE

SAMURAI'S

HEART

Walt Mussell

PROLOGUE

Haibara, Japan—August 1587

"By order of the regent, Christianity has been banned from the nation."

Sen shivered in her light silk kimono, her arms wrapped against her body. The mounted samurai directed his pronouncement toward her master, castle lord and regional governor Akamatsu Fumio. The mounted samurai, flanked by two more men on horseback, swept his icy stare over her and the rest of the servants and samurai. The meaning was clear. The pronouncement applied to everyone at Haibara Castle.

Behind the three horsemen, hundreds of additional samurai advanced on foot in the early sunlight, their long shadows as menacing as their numbers. The samurai were a token of the much larger force outside the gate and an indication of the fate that awaited all the castle servants if they didn't obey.

The three leaders dismounted. All three horsemen wore a gray *hakama*, the seven-pleated skirt of the samurai. A *kiri* flower, the crest of Regent Toyotomi, decorated their flowing blue robes. Did these men despise Christians or were they following orders? Sen bowed low and struggled to maintain a passive face as the men passed. The feelings of these men toward Christians didn't matter.

The samurai stopped in front of Lord Akamatsu, exchanged perfunctory bows with him, and then the tallest samurai pulled out a scroll. "Akamatsu-*sama*, you and your assemblage must renounce your faith."

Sen swallowed hard and glanced at Lord Akamatsu. Dressed in his fine golden kimono for the morning service, his regal bearing exuded confidence and peace. She laced her fingers and pressed her hands to her chin as she stared at the spectacle, drawing her arms in close.

Lord Akamatsu's voice rang across the keep: "I am a servant of Jesus Christ, the Son of God and the human pillar of the one true faith."

Stoic, the leader stared back. "The regent requests you reconsider. He reminds you of your great service to him over many campaigns. He does not wish to see it end."

Lord Akamatsu nodded, but his expression remained impassive. "I am grateful for his recognition. It does not have to end. Still, I am a follower of my God."

Sen's throat constricted as the words caused her heart to swell. The lead samurai's eyes widened. He rolled up the scroll, glancing at both the men with him before focusing on Lord Akamatsu. "Then, you are ordered to surrender your castle and lands."

"And if I refuse?"

The two flanking samurai stepped forward and drew their katanas, crossing the long swords at Lord Akamatsu's neck. "Then our forces will lay siege to your castle, lay waste to your grounds, and lay your Christian followers in their graves. We will eradicate this faith, starting with you."

A trickle of blood oozed from Lord Akamatsu's neck, and Sen gasped.

Lord Akamatsu's lips thinned, but he did not move. His gaze scanned both the servants and his own group of samurai nearby. His eyes conveyed love. "And if I accede? What happens to my people?"

"We will question each one of them. They will be

given the same chance as you. Renounce this foreign religion, and they may keep their station for whomever takes over the castle. Refuse, and they will face our judgment. Those we show mercy to may walk away with the clothes they wear. It is over. You are in our power now."

"If you have power over me, it's only because it was granted to you by God. I surrender the castle."

Pride welled inside Sen at Lord Akamatsu's steadfastness, and her arms relaxed as the samurai removed their swords from his neck. They spared him. But Sen's breath caught in her throat as the samurai faced the crowd.

"Line up," the lead man said, pointing in two directions. "Lord Akamatsu's samurai to the left side. His servants over here on the right."

Sen let the movement of the crowd carry her forward with the other servants. She bowed as more samurai passed, and then she headed to the servant line. She closed her eyes briefly. *Lord, please help us.*

A woman screamed, and the sound chilled Sen's soul. She craned her neck to see around the fifty or so people in front of her and watched in horror. A maid from the kitchen—it looked like she'd been first in line—fell to the ground. Blood poured from both sides of her neck. Her body convulsed, then grew still as the life flowed out of her. She was a young woman, only fifteen. Now she lay on the grass, her pale-green servant's kimono stained red.

Sen gulped air but could not swallow. She glanced around as best she could without moving her head. All of the servants' shoulders drooped. Would she and everyone in line face the same fate?

She finally managed to swallow, but the truth would not go down so easily. She was so close, so close. One more week, and then she would have left to be with her family. They needed her.

At the thought of her family, Sen reached into her

belt and sighed. It was still there, the letter from her mother telling Sen of the death of her sister, Haru. The crinkled feeling of the paper brought sadness. It also reminded her of her duty, the duty of a remaining sibling when an elder child had died. She must find a husband to marry into the family business and to help her look after her parents.

The line moved slowly. Maybe thirty people in front of her now. Sen's feet trembled with each step forward. Some people who had already stood before the samurai now walked free, staring at the ground, their chins tucked against their chests. Why had they been spared? Had they renounced Lord Akamatsu? Had they renounced Jesus? Were they now ashamed? Sen strained to hear, but the voices up front were inaudible despite the silence of the grounds. The samurai obviously meant for no one to listen. Sen leaned left but then righted herself. She would soon learn how the samurai offered mercy.

Another woman and then a man screamed and fell to the ground, blood draining from their necks and streaking their kimonos as they shook and then fell still. Two more people mercilessly slain. More servants walked past Sen, apparently headed to the castle entrance. Dejected with their heads bowed, they carried nothing but shame. Sen looked over at the other line, the line of samurai. Six men lay on the ground, motionless. Just as she might soon be. No screams had come from the samurai. Only the rank smell of death that floated on the air. Christians all, they'd refused suicide. None showed stomach wounds.

Sen craved water to quench her dry mouth. She struggled to breathe, each inhalation and exhalation sounding in her ears.

Could she make the right choice?

Confess God and leave her parents to Him? Renounce God to fulfill her duty to her family? Was that truly the choice set before her?

Sen wrung her hands as she drew closer to the front.

More of her fellow Christians fell to the ground. Still, she could not hear their words. Were people confessing God and still surviving?

Only ten people remained ahead of her in line. One of the samurai wiped his blade on a dead servant's kimono, then kicked some of the bodies to the side. Sen's knees and shoulders wobbled as the sun reflected off the metal, stinging her eyes with its harsh light.

A sword. The realization dawned on her. She would die by a sword.

Childhood memories rushed forward like rapids, bringing images of her parents to mind. Her father was the best swordsmith in her hometown of Himeji. He had crafted hundreds of swords over the years.

How would he feel if he were to learn his daughter was slain by one?

Sen grasped her belt and traced the edge of the letter with her fingertips. Duty to God. Duty to family. Her breathing grew steady. Measured. Calm.

She neared the front. One more person, an older woman, was ahead of her. The woman walked toward the three samurai awaiting her and bowed. Two of the samurai crossed their long swords at the woman's neck. The lead samurai's words finally reached Sen's ears. "I will say this once. Renounce your faith."

"I am a servant of Christ," the woman said.

Metal clanked against metal as the samurai completed the cut. The old woman's hands flew to her neck. Retching, she sank to her knees, then fell to the ground.

My turn.

Sen stepped forward and bowed to the three samurai, her gaze fixed on the bodies at her feet. Lives taken, cut down. The old woman before her twitched and inched toward Sen, the last flashes of her life ebbing away as the red spots of blood began to stain the hem of Sen's kimono. The coppery smell of blood filled Sen's nostrils. Bile rose in her throat as she choked back a gag and then straightened to her full height, her eyes focused on the samurai.

The men nodded back, then crossed their long swords at her neck. The cold metal dug into her skin, yet it burned like fire. Sweat poured down her face and back. The leader's face betrayed no mercy. "I will say this once. Renounce your faith."

Sen took in a shallow mouthful of air and exhaled. Tears bit her eyes as images of her parents' faces again rose in her mind.

God, please look after my family.

"I am a servant of Christ."

The blades bit deeper. The clank of swords sounded in Sen's ears as she struggled not to cry out. She scrunched her shoulders, bringing them up to salve the sting. Her head felt light and her knees buckled. Her breathing slowed . . . and then continued. Her dizziness cleared. She reached her hands to her neck and felt the hot liquid. The cuts were deep.

But she would live.

She rose slowly, too fearful to glance at the samurai's face, her eyes fighting tears. She should accept her fate and leave. It wasn't her place to ask, but she had to know. "Forgive me," she said, bowing low. "I beg your indulgence."

The samurai tilted his head, his gaze scanning her up and down. "You're the first to dare question us. You have courage, as misplaced as it may be. You may ask."

"Why?"

The lead samurai smiled. "You paused before you responded. You debated this religion in your mind. There is still hope for you."

Paused? She had paused?

She had prayed before she answered. The samurai had taken it for doubt. Her prayer had saved her.

"Thank you," she responded.

"Let the lesson burn into you. You survived today only by *our* justice. Now leave these grounds. See if your deity protects you."

Sen bowed, glanced once more at the bodies at her feet, and then walked toward the entrance. The castle gate, long a source of comfort, appeared ominous as she approached it. Just a few more strides and she'd be outside. Once outside, she would head for home.

But home was eighty miles away. Could she make it there on her own?

She passed through the gate, took a few steps along the road, and crashed to the ground.

About The Author

Walt Mussell lives in the Atlanta area with his wife and two sons. He works for a well-known corporation and writes in his spare time. Walt primarily writes historicals, with a focus on Japan, an interest he gained in the four years he lived there.

Outside of writing, his favorite activity is trying to keep up with his kids. As one is in college and one has graduated college and is actively looking for a job in his field, this is proving more difficult each day.

Please visit his website at www.waltmussell.com. Please follow him on Twitter at @wmussell and on Instagram at @authorwaltmussell. Please also check out his Facebook page at "Walt Mussell – Author" and check out his YouTube channel by searching for Walt Mussell to see his videos on Japanese Christian history.

Titles by Walt Mussell

A Second Chance - *Releasing August 2021*

The Samurai's Heart
(The Heart of the Samurai Book 1)

The Samurai's Honor
(The Heart of the Samurai Book 0)

Printed in Great Britain
by Amazon

33578579R00040